LET'S GO FOR A WALK OUTSIDE

D1397705

All rights reserved. Published by Scholastic Inc., *Publishers since 1920.* SCHOLASTIC and associated logos are trademarks and/or registered trademarks of Scholastic Inc.

ISBN 978-1-338-84713-0

10 9 8 7 6 5 4 3 2 1   23 24 25 26 27

Printed in the USA   40

First printing 2023

Book design by Elliane Mellet and Lauren Mowat

Scholastic Inc.

Let's go for a walk outside
and see what we can see.

Let's go for a walk outside
underneath the trees.

We can walk down
to the park . . .

. . . or walk around the block.

Walk, walk, walk, walk.
Look at that cute doggy!

Wow! It's a bluebird!

Walk, walk, walk, walk.
There goes a squirrel!

Let's collect some leaves!

Let's go for a walk outside
and see what we can see.

Let's go for a walk outside
underneath the trees.

We can walk down to the park or walk around the block.

Let's go for a walk outside.
Come on, let's take a walk!

Walk, walk, walk, walk.
Look at those bugs!

Let's collect some rocks!

**Walk, walk, walk, walk.
Look! What do you see?**

Here, hold my hand!

Let's go for a walk outside
and see what we can see.

Let's go for a walk outside underneath the trees.

We can walk down to the park
or walk around the block.

Let's go for a walk outside.
Come on . . .

Let's take a walk!